laura vaccaro seeger

green

A NEAL PORTER BOOK

ROARING BROOK PRESS

NEW YORK

forest green

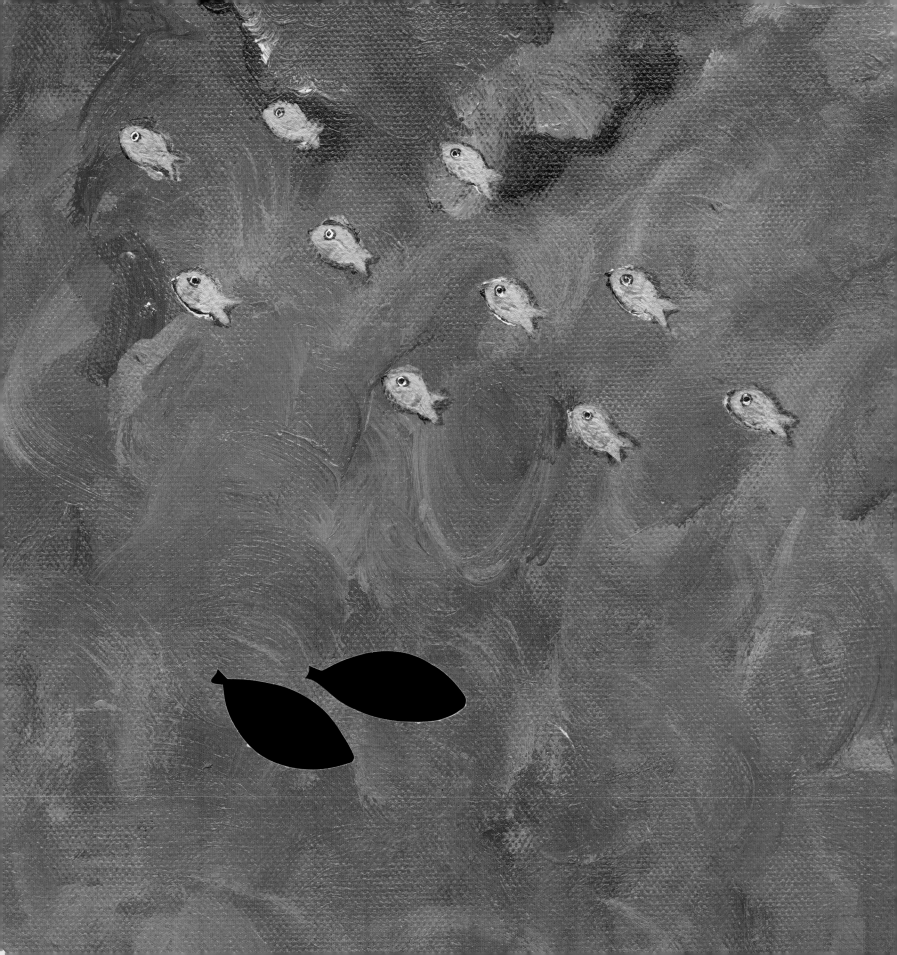

sea green

lime green

pea green

 green

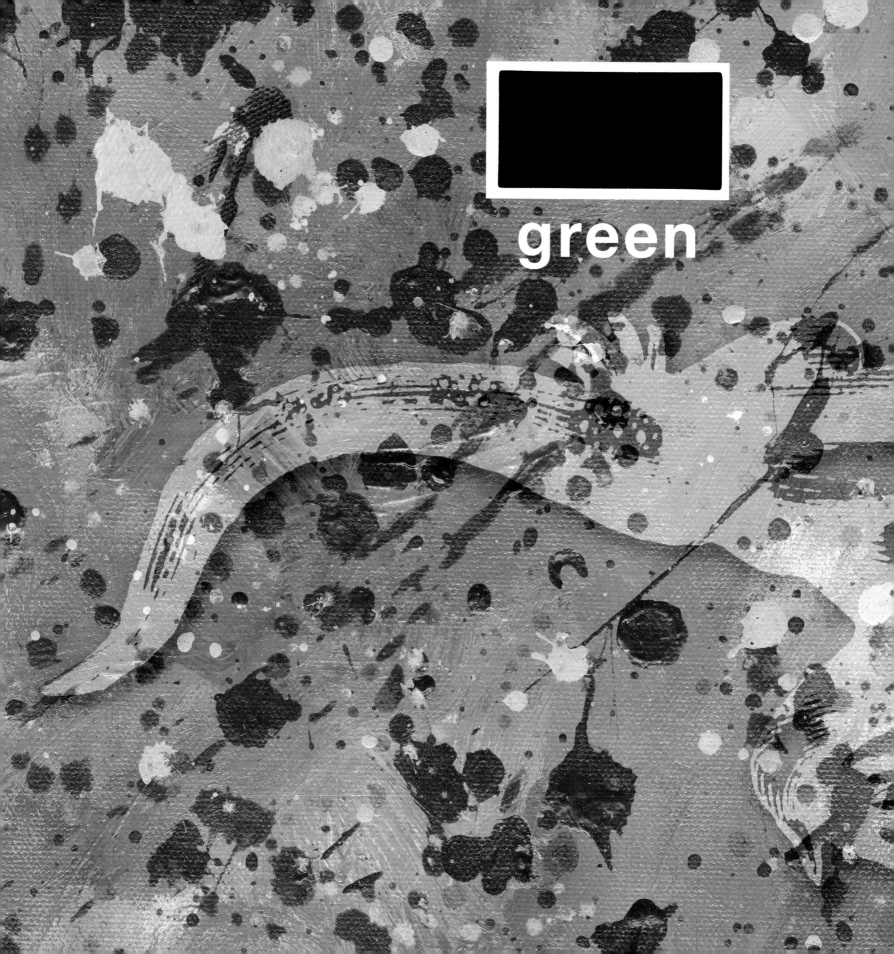

green

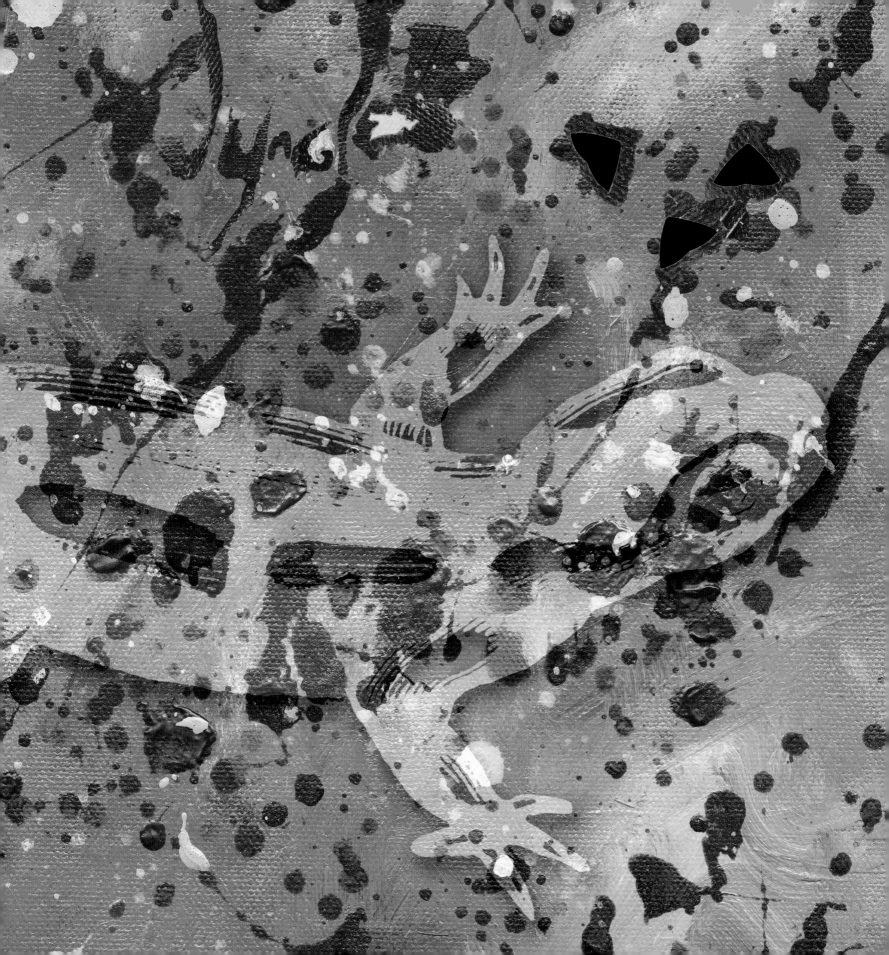

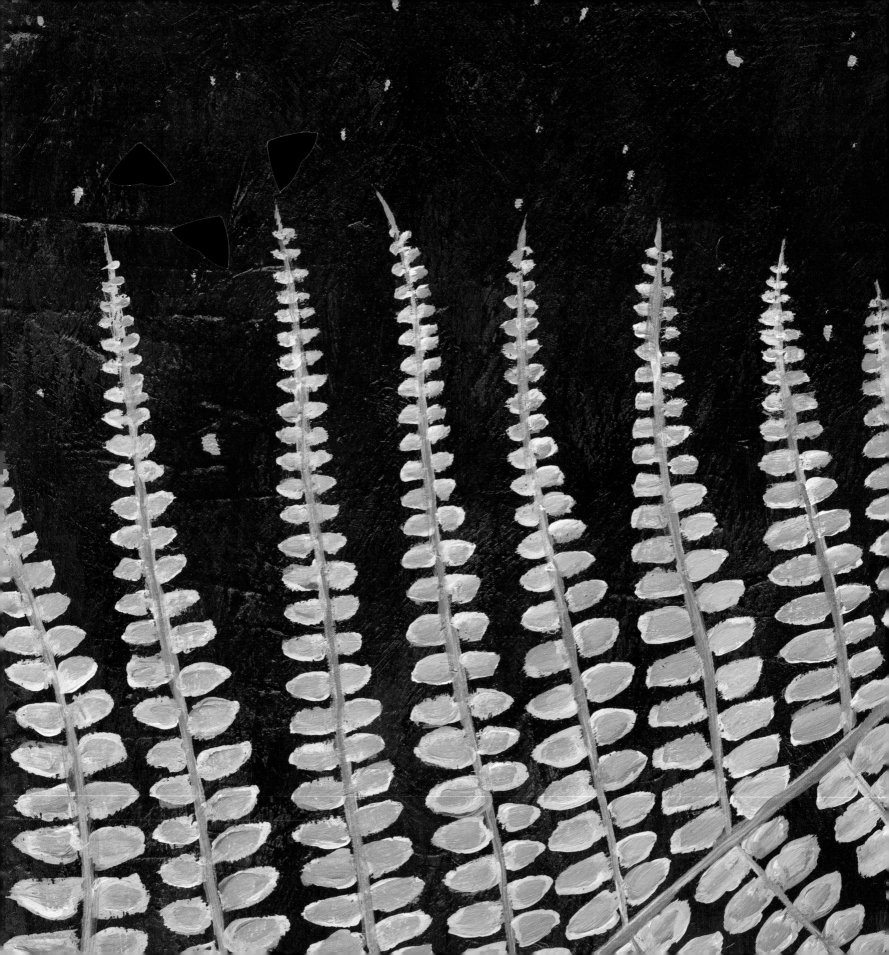

fern green

wacky
green

slow green

glow green

shaded green

all green

never green

no green

forever green

for judes

Copyright © 2012 by Laura Vaccaro Seeger

A Neal Porter Book

Published by Roaring Brook Press

Roaring Brook Press is a division of Holtzbrinck Publishing Holdings Limited Partnership

175 Fifth Avenue, New York, New York 10010

mackids.com

Library of Congress Cataloging-in-Publication Data

Seeger, Laura Vaccaro.
 Green / Laura Vaccaro Seeger. — 1st ed.
   p. cm.
 "A Neal Porter Book."
 Summary: Illustrations and simple, rhyming text explore the many shades of the color green.
 ISBN 978-1-59643-397-7
 [1. Stories in rhyme. 2. Green—Fiction.] I. Title.
 PZ8.3.S4504Gre 2012
 [E]—dc23

                                                                2011013495

Roaring Brook Press books are available for special promotions and premiums.
For details contact: Director of Special Markets, Holtzbrinck Publishers.

First edition 2012

Printed in the United States of America by Worzalla, Stevens Point, Wisconsin.

3   5   7   9   8   6   4